S0-BBZ-488

Benton Elementary School
68350 C.R. 31
Goshen, IN 46526

For Linda — wherever you are
—J. P. L.

For my personal La-di-da Daisy and Honeypot Crew,
who invite me daily to come play . . . and stay.
With love,
—D. C. B.

Atheneum Books for Young Readers
An imprint of Simon & Schuster
Children's Publishing Division
1230 Avenue of the Americas
New York, New York 10020
Text copyright © 1997 by J. Patrick Lewis
Illustrations copyright © 1997 by Diana Cain Bluthenthal
All rights reserved including the right of reproduction in
whole or in part in any form.
Book design by Becky Terhune
The text of this book is set in Bembo.
The illustrations are rendered in gouache.
First Edition
Printed in the United States of America
10 9 8 7 6 5 4 3 2 1
Library of Congress Cataloging-in-Publication Data
Lewis, J. Patrick.
The la-di-da hare / by J. Patrick Lewis ; illustrated by
Diana Cain Bluthenthal.—1st ed.
Summary: Honeypot Bear and Commodore Mouse sail to
the Island of Oh to visit the La-Di-Da Hare.
ISBN 0-689-31925-8
[1. Bears—Fiction. 2. Mice—Fiction. 3. Hares—Fiction.
4. Islands—Fiction. 5. Stories in rhyme.]
I. Bluthenthal, Diana Cain, ill. II. Title.
PZ8.3.L5855Lad   1997
[Fic]—dc20
95-44674

The La-di-da Hare

by J. Patrick Lewis

illustrated by

Diana Cain Bluthenthal

Atheneum Books for Young Readers

"Have you ever gone down to the Island of Oh?"
Said the Mouse to the Honeypot Bear,
"To hear the applause of Red Lobster claws
For the beautiful La-di-da Hare?

"She sits on the seashore, admiring the view—
If *you* were the La-di-da Hare, you would too—
For what would a Hare or a Bear rather do
   Than admire the highland,
   The blue butterflyland,
   The fabulous Island of Oh?"

"Dear me, dear Mouse!" cried the Honeypot Bear,
    "What a perfectly naughtical trip!
A walloping ride on the tropical tide,
    But what shall we do for a ship?"

"Pretend I'm your Captain—the Commodore Mouse
    Of the S.S. *Honeypot Bear*!"
Then he ran up the deck of the Honey Bear's neck,
    And they sailed through the sea-salt air.

As porpoises flipped over waterspout whales,
  The tiniest "Thar she blows!"
Came from the Commodore Mouse on the bridge
  Of the S.S. *Honeypot*'s nose.

They paddled by paw for a week without speaking,
They twiddled their toes in the silence of night,
Except when the Commodore Mouse took to squeaking
Commands from the bridge, such as "HONEY! Bear right!"

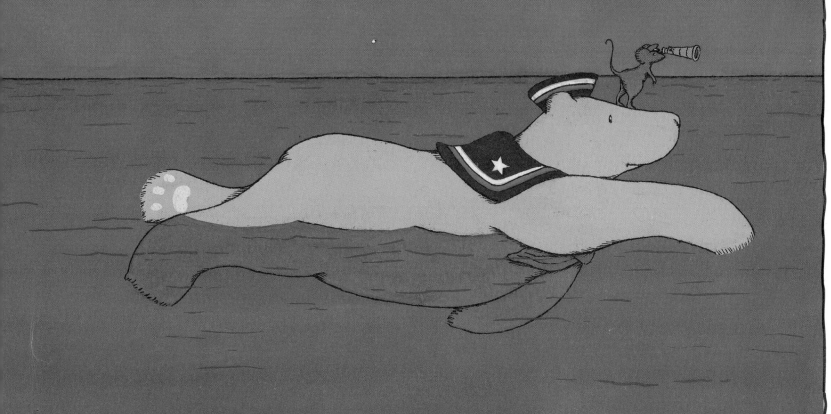

There! Over the ocean! Lovely Oh beaches
Of white sand—bananas—a coconut tree!
The Commodore, writing his welcoming speeches,
Remembered one curious fact. Said he:

"Did I mention, dear Bear,
The inhabitants there
Are especially fond of a vowel?
Flamingos *tra-la*
While the Peacocks *ahh-ha*
To *yoo-whoo* from the quizzical Owl!"

Benton Elementary School
68350 C.R. 31
Goshen, IN 46526

"Let the vowels begin!"
Said the Bear with a grin,
As he trotted along on the sand,
And he planted a spray
Of a seaweed bouquet
In her Ladyship La-di-da's hand.

La-di-da was heard to say,
As the Lobsters clapped away,
   "La-dee-dee and whoop-de-do!
   Oh, the Island, welcomes you!"

Commodore and Bear made bold,
Kissed her ring (2-carrot gold).
Lady Hare broke into song,
   "This is where you boys belong—
   The Oh trio by the sea!
   Pelicans, come pour the tea
   For Bear and Mouse and me!"

Snapping Turtles much preferred
Spreading gossip that they'd heard
From the rowdy Oyster crowd
Tittle-tattling out loud.

But the secrets they were telling
Were not nearly so compelling
As the sight of Lady Hare
Flirting with a Honey Bear!

"I once met a Duke and Duchess,
    And I've entertained a King,"
Cried the Lady from her lounge chair
    As she twirled her carrot ring.

"But I never knew a Commodore
    Or met a Honey Bear,
And I'd be delighted, fellas,
    If you'd slip into a pair

Of Bermuda shorts, Hawaiian shirts
    And cool designer shades,
Which is what Oh Island natives
    Wear to picnics and parades!"

Pink Flamingos, bright Blue Herons,
Gulls and Pelicans flew errands
    Out to sea and back to Oh—
Darting down the waves with daring,
Filling beaks with lox and herring
For the Hare who was preparing
    Deli sandwiches to go.

There, beside a charcoal griddle,
Mouse, re-reading *Stuart Little*,
    Sniffled in a tissue square.
When the sudden smell of Oyster—
Was it girl? Or was it boyster?—
Made his eyeballs all the moister,
    Commodore ran after Bear.

The Lobsters in their Lobster bibs,
The Oysters, underfed,
Hurried to place an order when
The La-di-da Hare said,

"Now who wants hot pastrami served
On pumpernickel rye?"
The Crocodile unzipped a smile
And then he snapped, "Aye-aye!"

"And who prefers a pat of peanut
  Butter on a bun?"
The Owls sat think-blinking that
  Might do. *"Yoo-whoo!"* said one.

"Who else would like some deviled eggs,
  Dill pickle on the side?"
"Ack-ack!" a Blue-clawed Crab clacked back,
  "Oi-oi!" the Oysters cried.

Then Honey Bear asked Commodore,
   Tucked safely in his shirt
(For Crocodile seemed much inclined
   To Commodore dessert!),

"Do you suppose they're having as
   Much fun as you and I?"
"*Ack-ack!*" the Island echoed back,
   "*Yoo-whoo!*" "*Oi-oi!*" "*Aye-aye!*"

Parrots and Owls,
Conversing in vowels,
Were comfortably settled and fed,
When the La-di-da rose
On her Q-Tip toes,
And this is the letter she read:

If I were the custard, my Honeypot Bear,
And you were a chocolaty chocolate eclair,
We'd break all the hearts
Of the cinnamon tarts,
Me and my Honeypot Bear.

If you were gold buttons, my Commodore Mouse,
And I were the cuff of an organdy blouse,
We'd flutter a sleeve
That you wouldn't believe,
Me and my Commodore Mouse.

A Gold-button Mouse on the Chocolate-ship Bear
Should never set sail on the sea-salt air!
Oh, stay with me please,
For crackers and cheese!

Forever, the La-di-da Hare

"Cheese?" shouted Commodore.
   "Crackers?" cried Bear.
"I wish you would stay,"
   Said the La-di-da Hare,
"For animal crackers
   And wheels of bleu cheese—
And a bungalow, boys,
   For as long as you please!"

Bear rose from his hammock
  And took Mouse's hand.
They walked with the Hare
  Down the cinnamon sand.
Then they wiggled their toes
  In waves on the shore,
And the S.S. *Honeypot*
  Sailed no more.

If you ever go down to the Island of Oh,
  You must visit the La-di-da Hare!
Her hutch of a house isn't much of a house,
  But the La-di-da doesn't much care. . . .

She sits on the seashore, admiring the view
With a beachcomber Bear and his Commodore crew!
For what would a Hare or that pair rather do
      Than admire the highland
      The blue butterflyland
      The fabulous Island of Oh?

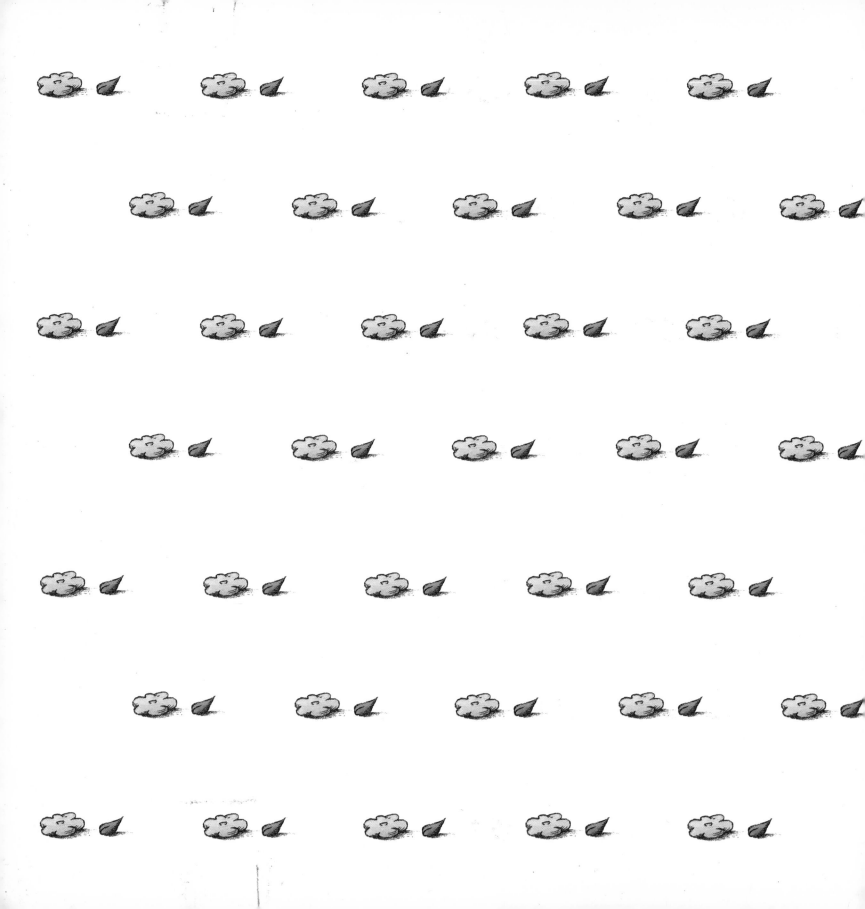